A Silly, Sticky Problem

adapted by **Patty Michaels**
based on the screenplay **"A Silly Sticky Situation"**
written by **Adam Rudman**

Ready-to-Read

Simon Spotlight
New York London Toronto Sydney New Delhi

SIMON SPOTLIGHT
An imprint of Simon & Schuster Children's Publishing Division
1230 Avenue of the Americas, New York, New York 10020
This Simon Spotlight edition May 2023

Donkey Hodie is produced by Fred Rogers Productions and Spiffy Pictures.

Manufactured in the United States of America 0623 LAK
10 9 8 7 6 5 4 3 2
ISBN 978-1-6659-3329-2 (hc)
ISBN 978-1-6659-3328-5 (pbk)
ISBN 978-1-6659-3330-8 (ebook)

Donkey Hodie skipped along happily.

“Big art! Going to make some big art,” she sang.

Just then Donkey ran into Clyde the Cloud.

"Where are you going with that giant crayon?" he asked.

'I am going to use it for
Big Art Day!" Donkey cheered.
'Oh fun! I should float on,"
Clyde said. "The forecast calls
for me to rain, and I do not
want to rain on your art!"

Donkey needed to get ready
for Big Art Day.
But as she tried to move
a giant, sticky bottle of glue,

one of her hooves got stuck to it!

Never fear! I have a trusty

way to solve this sticky

problem," she said.

Donkey used her free hoof
to pull her stuck hoof
off the bottle.
“The old hoof-pull trick
works every time,” she said.

Donkey got back to work. But as she tried to move the bottle of glue again, this time two of her hooves got stuck!

“The old hoof pull will not work now,” Donkey said. “There has to be another way to solve this sticky problem!”

"Aha!" Donkey realized.

"I have two more hooves

I can use to pull myself off!"

She put her two other hooves up on the bottle to unstick herself. But then she became completely stuck!

"I sure do have a silly, sticky problem," Donkey said.

Just then Duck Duck walked by.

"Hey, hey, Big Art Day!" she said. She looked at Donkey curiously. "Oh, Donkey. What is this about?"

"My hooves are stuck to the glue," Donkey admitted.

"I have a trusty way to solve this sticky problem. Wing power!" Duck Duck said.

Duck Duck climbed on Donkey and flapped her wings to pull Donkey off. Her trusty trick worked!

“Thank you! I am so glad
there was another way
to solve this sticky problem!”
Donkey said.

"It is finally time for . . .

. . . Big Art Day!" they cheered.

Want to help me move this
ig marker?" Donkey asked.

ut the marker was so heavy
hat Donkey and Duck Duck
ell . . . right onto the glue bottle.
Stuck again!" Donkey cried.

"Maybe you can pull me off,"

Donkey said.

'And then you can pull *me* off,"
)uck Duck added.
3ut that plan did not work.

Just then Bob Dog arrived.

"What are you doing?"

he asked.

"We both got stuck,"

Donkey admitted.

"Bow wow, I can help!"
Bob Dog said.
He used his "do anything"
bone to free his friends.

"Wow, that bone really can
do anything!" Donkey said.

Now it was time for . . .

Big Art!

But as the friends wondered what to make, they walked backward and fell right onto the bottle of glue!

Just then Purple Panda arrived and saw his three pals stuck to the glue.

"Hey-o, I know exactly what to do!" he said. "Join you in the 'stick to the big, sticky bottle of glue' game!"

He hopped onto the bottle of glue.

“We are not playing a game,” Duck Duck told Panda.

Now all four of us are stuck,"
said Bob Dog.
I, Donkey Hodie, will get us
unstuck," Donkey said.
Think, Donkey Hodie, think!"

Then Donkey remembered that when they got stuck in a muddy puddle, they were able to jump out of it!

"Let's try it!" they all said.

"One, two, three . . . JUMP!"

"If we stick together, we will get unstuck," Donkey sang.

"One, two, three . . . JUMP!" But that idea did not work.

"I wish we were near my pond," Duck Duck said. "The water would wash away the glue to help us get unstuck."

"Hee-haw, I have an idea!" Donkey said.

Then she called to Clyde the Cloud. "Clyde, could you rain down on us? Your rain will wash off this sticky glue!"

"Sure thing, Donkey!" Clyde said. And it worked! They were all unstuck!

As a thank-you, they made Clyde a giant card as their Big Art project!

"I love it!" said Clyde.

"Thanks for getting us unstuck, Clyde!" they cheered